Jessica's
First Prayer

by
Hesba Stretton

LAMPLIGHTER PUBLISHING
WAVERLY, PA

Jessica's First Prayer (Paperback Edition).
Copyright © 2013 by Lamplighter Publishing
All rights reserved.
Original Printing serialized in 1866.
First Printing, April 2013

Manufactured by Edwards Brothers, Lillington, NC, United
States of America, April 2013, 334079

Published by Lamplighter Publishing; a division of Lamplighter
Ministries International, Inc.

The *Lamplighter Collection* is a family collection of rare books
from the 17th, 18th and 19th centuries. Each edition is printed in
an attractive hard-bound collector's format. For more information,
call us at 1-570-585-1314, visit us at *www.lamplighter.net* or write:

     Lamplighter Publishing
     P.O. Box 777
     Waverly, PA 18471

Author: Hesba Stretton
Chief Editor: Mark Hamby
Copy Editors: Debra L. Nichols, Deborah Hamby, Darlene Catlett
Layout and Design: Kenn Anderson, Jr.
Cover Design: Abigail Lashbrook

ISBN: 1-58474-197-X
ISBN13: 978-1-58474-197-8

Preface.

Life's trials often become so overwhelming that sorrows numb our joy and diminish our faith. In this unforgettable story, little Jessica reminds us that we have a loving Father who delights in comforting His children and answering their prayers. Through her childlike faith our loveable, barefooted heroine teaches us that truly, there is nothing too difficult for the Lord.

Since 1866 *Jessica's First Prayer* has been instrumental in drawing countless children and adults to their loving Father. May this story now inspire *you* to pray and believe as Jessica did, that those who seek Him shall find Him, when they search for Him with all their hearts.

To Him be the glory forever,

Mark Hamby
Matthew 18:3

Publisher's note: The rules of punctuation, spelling, and even sentence structure of the 1800s were different than our present-day standards. We have chosen to keep the original format as much as possible, editing only when deemed necessary.

those who did could only discover that he kept the furniture of his stall at a neighbouring coffee-house, whither he wheeled his trestle and board and crockery every day, not later than half-past eight in the morning; after which he was wont to glide away with a soft footstep, and a mysterious and fugitive air, with many backward and sidelong glances, as if he dreaded observation, until he was lost among the crowds which thronged the streets. No one had ever had the preserving curiosity to track him all the way to his house, or to find out his other means of gaining a livelihood; but in general his stall was surrounded by customers whom he served with silent seriousness, and who did not grudge to pay him his charge for the refreshing coffee he supplied to them.

For several years the crowd of work-people had paused by the coffee-stall under the railway-arch, when one morning, in a partial lull of his business, the owner became suddenly aware of a pair of very bright dark eyes being fastened upon him and the slices of bread and butter on his board, with a gaze as hungry as that of a mouse which has been driven by famine into a trap. A thin and meagre face belonged to the eyes, which was half hidden by a mass of matted hair hanging over the forehead, and down the neck; the only covering which the head or neck had, for a tattered frock, scarcely fastened together with broken strings, was slipping down over the shivering shoulders of the little girl.

Stooping down to a basket behind his stall, he caught sight of two bare little feet curling up from the damp pavement, as the child lifted up first one and then the other and laid them one over another to gain a momentary feeling of warmth. Whoever the wretched child was, she did not speak; only at every steaming cupful which he poured out of his can, her dark eyes gleamed hungrily, and he could hear her smack her thin lips, as if in fancy she was tasting the warm and fragrant coffee.

"Oh, come now!" he said at last, when only one boy was left taking his breakfast leisurely, and he leaned over his stall to speak in a low and quiet tone; "why don't you go away, little girl? Come, come; you're staying too long, you know."

"I'm just going, sir," she answered, shrugging her small shoulders to draw her frock up higher about her neck: "only it's raining cats and dogs outside, and mother's been away all night, and she took the key with her; and it's so nice to smell the coffee; and the police has left off worriting[1] me while I've been here. He thinks I'm a customer taking my breakfast." And the little girl laughed a shrill little laugh of mockery at herself and the policeman.

---

[1] Worrying; annoying.

"You've had no breakfast, I suppose," said the coffee-stall keeper in the same low and confidential voice, and leaning over his stall till his face nearly touched the thin, sharp features of the child.

"No," she replied coolly, "and I shall want my dinner dreadful bad afore I get it, I know. You don't often feel dreadful hungry, do you, sir? I'm not griped yet, you know; but afore I taste my dinner it'll be pretty bad, I tell you. Ah! very bad indeed!"

She turned away with a knowing nod, as much as to say she had one experience in life to which he was quite a stranger; but before she had gone half a dozen steps, she heard the quiet voice calling to her in rather louder tones, and in an instant she was back at the stall.

"Slip in here," said the owner in a cautious whisper; "here's a little coffee left and a few crusts. There, you must never come again, you know. I never give to beggars; and if you begged, I'd have called the police. There, put your poor feet towards the fire. Now aren't you comfortable?"

The child looked up with a face of intense satisfaction. She was seated upon an empty basket with her feet near the pan of charcoal, and a cup of steaming coffee on her lap; but her mouth was too full for her to reply, except by a very deep nod, which expressed unbounded delight. The man was busy for a while packing up his crockery; but every now and then he stopped to look down upon her, and to shake his head gravely.

"What's your name?" he asked at length; "but there, never mind! I don't care what it is. What's your name to do with me, I wonder?"

"It's Jessica," said the girl; "but mother and everybody calls me Jess. You'd be tired of being called Jess, if you was me. It's Jess here, and Jess there; and everybody wanting me to

go on errands. And they think nothing of giving me smacks and kicks
and pinches. Look here!"

Whether her arms were black and
blue from the cold or from ill-usage, he
could not tell; but he shook his head
again seriously, and the child felt
encouraged to go on.

"I wish I could stay here for ever
and ever, just as I am!" she cried.
"But you're going away now; and am
I never to come again or you'll set the
police on me?"

"Yes," said the coffee-stall keeper,
very softly, and looking round to see
if there were any other ragged children within sight; "if you'll promise
not to come again for a whole week,
and not to tell anybody else, you may
come once more. I'll give you one other
treat. But you must be off now."

"I'm off, sir," she said sharply; "but
if you've an errand I could go on, I'd
do it all right, I would. Let me carry
some of your things."

"No, no," cried the man; "you run away, like a good girl; and mind! I'm not to see you again for a whole week."

"All right!" answered Jess, setting off down the rainy street at a quick run, as if to show her willing agreement to the bargain; while the coffee-stall keeper, with many a cautious glance around him, removed his stock-in-trade to the coffee-house near at hand, and was seen no more for the rest of the day in the neighbourhood of the railway-bridge.

Chapter II.

Jessica's Temptation.

ESSICA kept her part of the bargain faithfully; and though the solemn and silent man under the dark shadow of the bridge looked out for her every morning as he served his customers, he caught no glimpse of her wan[2] face and thin little frame. But when the appointed time was

---

[2]Unhealthily pale; ashen; pallid.

finished, she presented herself at the stall, with her hungry eyes fastened again upon the piles of buns and bread and butter, which were fast disappearing before the demands of the buyers. The business was at its height, and the famished child stood quietly on one side watching for the throng to melt away.

But as soon as the nearest church clock had chimed eight, she drew a little nearer to the stall, and at a signal from its owner she slipped between the trestles of his stand and took up her former position on the empty basket. To his eyes she seemed even a little thinner, and certainly more ragged, than before; and he laid a whole bun, a stale one which was left from yesterday's stock, upon her lap, as she lifted the cup of coffee to her lips with both her numbed hands.

"What's your name?" she asked, looking up to him with her keen eyes.

"Why?" he answered, hesitatingly, as if he was reluctant to tell so much of himself; "my name is Daniel."

"And where do you live, Mr. Dan'el?" she inquired.

"Oh, come now!" he exclaimed, "if you're going to be impudent, you'd better march off. What business is it of yours where I live? I don't want to know where you live, I can tell you."

"I didn't mean no offence," said Jess humbly, "only I thought I'd like to know where a good man like you lived. You're a very good man, aren't you, Mr. Dan'el?"

"I don't know," he answered uneasily; "I'm afraid I'm not."

"Oh, but you are, you know," continued Jess. "You make good coffee; prime! and buns too! And I've been watching you hundreds of times afore you saw me, and the police leaves you alone, and never tells you to move on. Oh, yes! you must be a very good man."

Daniel sighed and fidgeted about his crockery with a grave and occupied air, as if he were pondering over the child's notion of goodness. He made good coffee, and the police left him alone! It was quite true; yet still as he counted up the store of pence which had accumulated in his strong canvas bag, he sighed again still more heavily. He purposely let one of his pennies fall upon the muddy pavement, and went on counting the rest busily, while he furtively watched the little girl sitting at his feet.

Without a shade of change upon her small face, she covered the penny with her foot, and drew it in carefully towards her, while she continued to chatter fluently to him. For a moment a feeling of pain shot a pang through Daniel's heart; and then he congratulated himself on having entrapped the young thief. It was time to be leaving now; but before he went he would make her move her bare foot and disclose the penny concealed beneath it, and then he would warn her never to venture near his stall again. This was her gratitude, he thought; he had given her two breakfasts and more kindness than he had shown to any fellow-creature for many a long year; and, at the first chance, the young jade turned upon him and robbed him!

He was brooding over it painfully in his mind, when Jessica's uplifted face changed suddenly and a dark flush crept over her pale cheeks, and the tears started to her eyes. She stooped down and picked up the coin out of the mud; she rubbed it bright and clean upon her rags, and laid it upon the stall close to his hand, but without speaking a word. Daniel looked down upon her solemnly and searchingly.

"What's this?" he asked.

"Please, Mr. Dan'el," she answered, "it dropped, and you didn't hear it."

"Jess," he said sternly, "tell me all about it."

"Oh, please," she sobbed, "I never had a penny of my very own but once; and it rolled close to my foot; and you didn't see it; and I hid it up sharp; and then I thought how kind you'd been, and how good the coffee and buns are, and how you let me warm myself at your fire; and, please, I couldn't keep the penny any longer. You'll never let me come again, I guess."

Daniel turned away for a minute, busying himself with putting his cups and saucers into the basket, while Jessica stood by trembling, with the large tears rolling slowly down her cheeks. The snug, dark corner, with its warm fire of charcoal and its fragrant smell of coffee, had been a paradise to her for these two brief spans of time; but she had been guilty of the sin which would drive her from it. All beyond the railway-arch the streets stretched away, cold and dreary, with no friendly face to meet her; yet she was only lingering sorrowfully to hear the words spoken which should forbid her to return to this pleasant spot. Mr. Daniel turned round at last, and met her tearful gaze with a look of strange emotion upon his own solemn face.

"Jess," he said, "I could never have done it myself. But you may come here every Wednesday morning, as this is a Wednesday, and there'll always be a cup of coffee for you."

She thought he meant that he could not have hidden the penny under his foot, and she went away a little saddened and subdued, notwithstanding her great delight in the expectation of such a treat every week; while Daniel, pondering over the struggle that must have passed through her childish mind, went on his way, from time to time shaking his head, and muttering to himself, "I couldn't have done it myself; I never could have done it myself."

Chapter III.

An Old Friend in a New Dress.

EEK after week, through the last three months of the year, Jessica appeared every Wednesday at the coffee-stall, and, after waiting patiently till the close of the breakfasting business, received her pittance from the charity of her new friend. After a while Daniel allowed her to carry some of his load to the coffee-house,

but he never suffered her to follow far-
ther, and he was always particular to
watch her out of sight before he turned
off through the intricate mazes of the
streets in the direction of his own
home. Neither did he encourage her to
ask him any more questions; and often
but very few words passed between
them during Jessica's breakfast-time.

As to Jessica's home, she made no
secret of it, and Daniel might have followed her any time he pleased. It was
a single room which had once been a
hayloft over the stable of an old inn,
now in use for two or three donkeys,
the property of costermongers[3] dwelling in the court about it. The mode
of entrance was by a wooden ladder,
whose rungs were crazy and broken,
and which led up through a trap-door
in the floor of the loft. The interior of
the home was as desolate and comfort-
less as that of the stable below, with
only a litter of straw for the bedding,

---

[3] Those who sell fish or produce from carts or stands.

and a few bricks and boards for the
furniture.

Everything that could be pawned
had disappeared long ago, and Jessica's mother often lamented that she
could not thus dispose of her child. Yet
Jessica was hardly a burden to her. It
was a long time since she had taken
any care to provide her with food or
clothing, and the girl had to earn or
beg for herself the meat which kept a
scanty life within her. Jess was the
drudge and errand-girl of the court;
and what with being cuffed and beaten
by her mother, and over-worked and
ill-used by her numerous employers,
her life was a hard one. But now there
was always Wednesday morning to
count upon and look forward to; and
by-and-by a second scene of amazed
delight opened upon her.

Jessica had wandered far away
from home in the early darkness of
a winter's evening, after a violent
outbreak of her drunken mother,

and she was still sobbing now and
then, with long-drawn sobs of pain
and weariness, when she saw a little
way before her the tall, well-known
figure of her friend, Mr. Daniel. He
was dressed in a suit of black, with
a white neckcloth, and he was pacing
with brisk, yet measured, steps along
the lighted streets. Jessica felt afraid
of speaking to him, but she followed
at a little distance, until presently
he stopped before the iron gates of a
large building, and, unlocking them,
passed on to the arched door-way, and
with a heavy key opened the folding-
doors and entered in.

The child stole after him, but paused
for a few minutes, trembling upon the
threshold, until the gleam of a light
within tempted her to venture a few
steps forward, and to push a little way
open an inner door, covered with crimson baize,[4] only so far as to enable her
to peep through at the inside. Then,

---

[4] A soft fabric resembling felt or flannel.

growing bolder by degrees, she crept through herself, drawing the door noiselessly behind her. The place was in partial gloom, but Daniel was kindling every gaslight and each minute lit it up in more striking grandeur. She stood in a carpeted aisle, with high oaken pews on each side almost as black as ebony. A gallery of the same dark old oak ran around the walls, resting upon massive pillars, behind one of which she was partly concealed, gazing with eager eyes at Daniel as he mounted the pulpit steps and kindled the lights there, disclosing to her curious delight the glittering pipes of an organ behind it.

Before long the slow and soft-footed chapel keeper disappeared for a minute or two into a vestry; and Jessica, availing herself of this short absence, stole silently up under the shelter of the dark pews until she reached the steps of the organ loft, with its golden show. But at this moment Mr. Daniel appeared again, arrayed in a long gown of black serge;[5] and as she stood spell-bound gazing at the strange appearance of her patron, his eyes fell upon her, and he also was struck speechless for a minute, with an air of amazement and dismay upon his grave face.

"Come now," he exclaimed harshly, as soon as he could recover his presence of mind, "you must take yourself out of this. This isn't any place for such as you. It's for ladies and gentlemen; so you must run away sharp before anybody comes. How ever did you find your way here?"

He had come very close to her, and bent down to whisper in her ear, looking nervously round to the entrance all the time. Jessica's eager tongue was loosened.

"Mother beat me," she said, "and turned me into the streets, and I saw you there, so I followed you up. I'll run

---

[5] A strong cloth, usually made of wool.

away this minute, Mr. Dan'el; but it's a nice place. What do the ladies and gentlemen do when they come here? Tell me, and I'll be off sharp."

"They come here to pray," whispered Daniel.

"What is pray?" asked Jessica.

"Bless the child!" cried Daniel, in perplexity. "Why, they kneel down in those pews—most of them sit, though; and the minister up in the pulpit tells God what they want."

Jessica gazed into his face with such an air of bewilderment that a faint smile crept over the sedate features of the pew-opener.

"What is a minister and God?" she said; "and do ladies and gentlemen want anything? I thought they'd everything they wanted, Mr. Dan'el."

"Oh!" cried Daniel, "you must be off, you know. They'll be coming in a minute, and they'd be shocked to see a ragged little heathen like you. This is the pulpit, where the minister stands and preaches to 'em; and there are the pews where they sit to listen to him, or to go to sleep, maybe; and that's the organ to play music to their singing. There, I've told you everything, and you must never come again, never."

"Mr. Dan'el," said Jessica, "I don't know nothing about it. Isn't there a dark little corner somewhere that I could hide in?"

"No, no," interrupted Daniel, impatiently; "we couldn't do with such a little heathen, with no shoes or bonnet on. Come now, it's only a quarter to the time, and somebody will be here in a minute. Run away, do!"

Jessica retraced her steps slowly to the crimson door, casting many a longing look backwards; but Mr. Daniel stood at the end of the aisle, frowning upon her whenever she glanced behind. She gained the lobby at last, but already someone was approaching the chapel door, and beneath the lamp at the gate stood one of her natural enemies—a policeman. Her heart beat fast, but she was quick-witted, and in another instant she spied a place of concealment behind one of the doors, into which she crept for safety until the path should be clear and the policeman passed upon his beat.

The congregation began to arrive quickly. She heard the rustling of silk dresses, and she could see the gentlemen and ladies pass by the niche between the door and the post. Once she ventured to stretch out a thin little finger and touch a velvet mantle as the wearer of it swept by, but no one caught her in the act, or suspected her presence behind the door.

Mr. Daniel, she could see, was very busy ushering the people to their seats; but there was a startled look lingering upon his face, and every now and then he peered anxiously into the outer gloom and darkness, and even once called to the policeman to ask if he had seen a ragged child hanging about.

After a while the organ began to sound, and Jessica, crouching down in her hiding-place, listened entranced to the sweet music. She could not tell what made her cry, but the tears came so rapidly that it was of no use to rub the corners of her eyes with her hard knuckles: so she lay down upon the ground, and buried her face in her hands, and wept without restraint. When the singing was over, she could only catch a confused sound of a voice speaking.

The lobby was empty now, and the crimson doors closed. The policeman, also, had walked on. This was the moment to escape. She raised herself from the ground with a feeling of weariness and sorrow; and, thinking sadly of the light, and warmth, and music that were within the closed doors, she stepped out into the cold and darkness of the streets, and loitered homewards with a heavy heart.

Chapter IV.

Peeps Into the Church.

T was not the last time that Jessica concealed herself behind the baize-covered door. She could not overcome the urgent desire to enjoy again and again the secret and perilous pleasure, and Sunday after Sunday she watched in the dark streets for the moment when she could slip in unseen. She soon learned the

exact time when Daniel would be
occupied in lighting up, before the
policeman would take up his station
at the entrance, and, again, the very
minute at which it would be wise and
safe to take her departure.

Sometimes the child laughed noiselessly to herself, until she shook with
suppressed merriment, as she saw
Daniel standing unconsciously in
the lobby, with his solemn face and
grave air, to receive the congregation,
much as he faced his customers at the
coffee-stall. She learned to know the
minister by sight—the tall, thin, pale
gentleman, who passed through a side
door with his head bent as if in deep
thought, while two little girls, about
her own age, followed him with sedate
yet pleasant faces.

Jessica took a great interest in the
minister's children. The young one
was fair, and the elder was about as
tall as herself, and had eyes and hair
as dark; but oh, how cared for, how

plainly waited on by tender hands! Sometimes, when they were gone by, she would close her eyes, and wonder what they would do in one of the high black pews inside, where there was no place for a ragged, barefooted girl like her; and now and then her wonderings almost ended in a sob, which she was compelled to stifle.

It was an untold relief to Daniel that Jessica did not ply him with questions, as he feared, when she came for breakfast every Wednesday morning; but she was too shrewd and cunning for that. She wished him to forget that she had ever been there, and by-and-by her wish was accomplished, and Daniel was no longer uneasy, while he was lighting the lamps, with the dread of seeing the child's wild face starting up before him.

But the light evenings of summer-time were drawing near apace, and Jessica foresaw, with dismay, that her Sunday treat would soon be over.

The risk of discovery increased every week, for the sun was later and later in setting, and there would be no chance of creeping in and out unseen in the broad daylight. Already it needed both watchfulness and alertness to dart in at the right moment in the grey twilight; but still she could not give it up; and if it had not been for the fear of offending Mr. Daniel, she would have resolved upon going until she was found out. They could not punish her very much for standing in the lobby of a chapel.

Jessica was found out, however, before the dusky evenings were quite gone. It happened one night that the minister's children, coming early to the chapel, saw a small tattered figure, bareheaded and barefooted, dart swiftly up the steps before them and disappear within the lobby. They paused and looked at one another, and then, hand in hand, their hearts beating quickly, and the colour coming and going on their faces, they followed this strange new member of their father's congregation. The pew-opener was nowhere to be seen, but their quick eyes detected the prints of the wet little feet which had trodden the clean pavement before them, and in an instant they discovered Jessica crouching behind the door.

"Let us call Daniel Standring," said Winny, the younger child, clinging to her sister; but she had spoken aloud, and Jessica overheard her, and before they could stir a step she stood before them with an earnest and imploring face.

"Oh, don't have me drove away," she cried; "I'm a very poor little girl, and it's all the pleasure I've got. I've seen you lots of times, with that tall gentleman as stoops, and I didn't think you'd have me drove away. I don't do any harm behind the door, and if

Mr. Dan'el finds me out he won't give me any more coffee."

"Little girl," said the elder child, in a composed and demure voice, "we don't mean to be unkind to you; but what do you come here for, and why do you hide yourself behind the door?"

"I like to hear the music," answered Jessica, "and I want to find out what pray is, and the minister and God. I know it's only for ladies and gentle-men, and fine children like you; but I'd like to go inside just for once, and see what you do."

"You shall come with us into our pew," cried Winny, in an eager and impulsive tone; but Jane laid her hand upon her outstretched arm with a glance at Jessica's ragged clothes and matted hair. It was a question difficult enough to perplex them. The little outcast was plainly too dirty and neglected for them to invite her to sit side by side with them in their crimson-lined pew, and no poor people attended the chapel with whom she could have a seat. But Winny, with flushing cheeks and indignant eyes, looked reproachfully at her elder sister.

"Jane," she said, opening her Testament and turning over the leaves hurriedly, "this was papa's text a little while ago: 'For if there come unto your assembly a man with a gold ring, in goodly apparel, and there come in also a poor man in vile raiment; and ye have respect to him that weareth the gay clothing, and say unto him, "Sit thou here in a good place;" and say to the poor, "Stand thou here," or "Sit here under my footstool," are ye not then partial in yourselves, and are become judges of evil thoughts?"[6] If we don't take this little girl into our pew, we don't 'have the faith of our Lord Jesus Christ, the Lord of glory, with respect of persons.'"[7]

---

[6] James 2:2-4
[7] Referring to James 2:1.

"I don't know what to do," answered Jane, sighing; "the Bible seems plain; but I'm sure papa would not like it. Let us ask the chapel-keeper."

"Oh, no, no!" cried Jessica; "don't let Mr. Dan'el catch me here. I won't come again, indeed; and I'll promise not to try and find out about God and the minister, if you'll only let me go."

"But, my little girl," said Jane, in a sweet but grave manner, "we ought to teach you about God, if you don't know Him. Our papa is the minister, and if you'll come with us we'll ask him what we must do."

"Will Mr. Dan'el see me?" asked Jessica.

"Nobody but papa is in the vestry," answered Jane, "and he'll tell us all, you and us, what we ought to do. You'll not be afraid of him, will you?"

"No," said Jessica cheerfully, following the minister's children as they led her along the side of the chapel towards the vestry.

"He is not such a terrible personage," said Winny, looking round encouragingly, as Jane tapped softly at the door, and they heard a voice saying, "Come in."

Chapter V.

A New World Opens.

HE minister was sitting in an easy-chair before a comfortable fire, with a hymn-book in his hand, which he closed as the three children appeared in the open door-way. Jessica had seen his pale and thoughtful face many a time from her hiding-place, but she had never met the keen, earnest, searching gaze of his eyes,

which seemed to pierce through all
her wretchedness and misery, and to
read at once the whole history of her
desolate life. But before her eyelids
could droop, or she could drop a rev-
erential curtsey, the minister's face
kindled with a glow of pitying tenderness and compassion; as she fastened
her eyes upon him, he gave her new
heart and courage. His children ran
to him, leaving Jessica upon the mat
at the door, and with eager voices and
gestures told him the difficulty they
were in.

"Come here, little girl," he said; and
Jessica walked across the carpeted
floor till she stood right before him,
with folded hands, and eyes that
looked frankly into his.

"What is your name, my child?" he
asked.

"Jessica," she answered.

"Jessica," he repeated with a smile;
"that is a strange name."

"Mother used to play 'Jessica' at the

theatre, sir," she said, "and I used to be a fairy in the pantomime, till I grew too tall and ugly. If I'm pretty when I grow up, mother says I shall play too; but I've a long time to wait. Are you the minister, sir?"

"Yes," he answered, smiling again.

"What is a minister?" she inquired.

"A servant!" he replied, looking away thoughtfully into the red embers of the fire.

"Papa!" cried Jane and Winny, in tones of astonishment; but Jessica gazed steadily at the minister, who was now looking back again into her bright eyes.

"Please, sir, whose servant are you?" she asked.

"The servant of God and of man," he answered solemnly. "Jessica, I am your servant."

The child shook her head, and laughed shrilly as she gazed round the room, and at the handsome clothing of the minister's daughters, while she drew her rags closer about her, and shivered a little, as if she felt a sting of the east wind, which was blowing keenly through the streets. The sound of her shrill, childish laugh made the minister's heart ache and the tears burn under his eyelids.

"Who is God?" asked the child. "When mother's in a good temper, sometimes she says, 'God bless me!' Do you know Him, please, minister?"

But before there was time to answer, the door into the chapel was opened, and Daniel stood upon the threshold. At first he stared blandly forwards, but then his grave face grew ghastly pale, and he laid his hand upon the door to support himself until he could recover his speech and senses. Jessica also looked about her, scared and irresolute, as if anxious to run away or to hide herself. The minister was the first to speak.

"Jessica," he said, "there is a place close under my pulpit where you shall sit, and where I can see you all the time. Be a good girl and listen, and you will hear something about God. Standring, put this little one in front of the pews by the pulpit steps."

Before she could believe it, Jessica found herself inside the chapel, facing the glittering organ, from which a sweet strain of music was sounding. Not far from her, Jane and Winny were peeping over the front of their pew, with friendly smiles and glances. It was evident that the minister's elder daughter was anxious about her behavior, and she made energetic signs to her when to stand up and when to kneel; but Winny was content with smiling at her whenever her head rose above the top of the pew.

Jessica was happy, but not in the least abashed.[8] The ladies and gentlemen were not at all unlike those whom she had often seen when she was a fairy at the theatre; and very soon

---

[8] Ashamed; embarrassed.

her attention was engrossed by the
minister, whose eyes often fell upon
her as she gazed eagerly, with uplifted
face, upon him. She could scarcely
understand a word of what he said,
but she liked the tones of his voice,
and the tender pity of his face as he
looked down upon her. Daniel hovered
about a good deal, with an air of un-
easiness and displeasure, but she was
unconscious of his presence. Jessica
was intent upon finding out what a
minister and God were.

Chapter VI.

The First Prayer.

HEN the service was ended, the minister descended the pulpit steps, just as Daniel was about to hurry Jessica away, and taking her by the hand in the face of all the congregation, he led her into the vestry, whither Jane and Winny quickly followed them. He was fatigued with the services of the day, and his pale face was paler than ever as he placed Jessica before his chair, into which he threw himself with an air of exhaustion; bowing his head upon his hands, he said in a low but clear tone, "Lord, these are the lambs of Thy flock. Help me to feed Thy lambs!"

"Children," he said, with a smile upon his weary face, "it is no easy thing to know God. But this one thing we know, that He is our Father—my Father and your Father, Jessica. He loves you, and cares for you more than I do for my little girls here."

He smiled at them and they at him, with an expression which Jessica felt and understood, though it made her sad. She trembled a little, and the minister's ear caught the sound of a faint though bitter sob.

"I never had any father," she said, sorrowfully.

"God is your Father," he answered very gently; "He knows all about you, because He is present everywhere. We cannot see Him, but we have only to speak and He hears us, and we may ask Him for whatever we want."

"Will He let me speak to Him as well as these fine children that are clean and have got nice clothes?" asked Jessica, glancing anxiously at her muddy feet and her soiled and tattered frock.

"Yes," said the minister, smiling, yet sighing at the same time; "you may ask Him this moment for what you want."

Jessica gazed round the room with large, wide-open eyes, as if she were seeking to see God; but then she shut her eyelids tightly, and bending her head upon her hands, as she had seen the minister do, she said, "Oh, God! I want to know about You. And please pay Mr. Dan'el for all the warm coffee he's given."

Jane and Winny listened with faces

of unutterable amazement; but the tears stood in the minister's eyes, and he added "Amen" to Jessica's first prayer.

Chapter VII.

Hard Questions.

ANIEL had no opportunity of speaking to Jessica; for, after waiting until the minister left the vestry, he found that she had gone away by the side entrance. He had to wait, therefore, until Wednesday morning, and the sight of her pinched little face was welcome to him when he saw it looking wistfully over the coffee-stall.

Yet he had made up his mind to forbid her to come again, and to threaten her with the policeman if he ever caught her at the chapel, where, for the future, he intended to keep a sharper lookout. But before he could speak, Jessica had slipped under the stall and taken her old seat upon the up-turned basket.

"Mr. Dan'el," she said, "has God paid you for my sups of coffee yet?"

"Paid me?" he repeated; "God? No."

"Well, He will," she answered, nodding her head sagely; "don't you be afraid of your money, Mr. Dan'el; I've asked Him a many times, and the minister says He's sure to do it."

"Jess," said Daniel sternly, "have you been and told the minister about my coffee-stall?"

"No," she answered, with a beaming smile, "but I've told God lots and lots of times since Sunday, and He's sure to pay in a day or two."

"Jess," continued Daniel, more gently, "you're a sharp little girl, I see;

and now, mind, I'm going to trust you.
You're never to say a word about me
or my coffee-stall; because the folks at
our chapel are very grand, and might
think it low and mean[9] of me to keep
a coffee-stall. Very likely they'd say I
mustn't be chapel-keeper any longer,
and I should lose a deal of money."

"Why do you keep the stall, then?"
asked Jessica.

"Don't you see what a many pennies
I get every morning?" he said, shaking his canvas bag. "I get a good deal
of money that way in a year."

"What do you want such a deal of
money for?" she inquired; "do you give
it to God?"

Daniel did not answer, but the
question went to his heart like a
sword-thrust. What did he want so
much money for? He thought of his one
bare solitary room, where he lodged
alone, a good way from the railway-
bridge, with very few comforts in it,

---

[9] Of low social position.

but containing a desk, strongly and securely fastened, in which was his savings-bank book and his receipts for money put out at interest, and a bag of sovereigns, for which he had been toiling and slaving both on Sundays and week-days. He could not remember giving anything away, except the dregs of the coffee and the stale buns, for which Jessica was asking God to pay him. He coughed and cleared his throat, and rubbed his eyes; and then, with nervous and hesitating fingers, he took a penny from his bag and slipped it into Jessica's hand.

"No, no, Mr. Dan'el," she said; "I don't want you to give me any of your pennies. I want God to pay you."

"Ay, He'll pay me," muttered Daniel; "there'll be a day of reckoning by-and-by."

"Does God have reckoning days?" asked Jessica. "I used to like reckoning days when I was a fairy."

"Ay, ay," he answered; "but there's few folks like God's reckoning days."

"But you'll be glad, won't you?" she said.

Daniel bade her get on with her breakfast, and then he turned over in his mind the thoughts which her questions had awakened. Conscience told him he would not be glad to meet God's reckoning day.

"Mr. Dan'el," said Jessica, when they were about to separate, and he would not take back his gift of a penny, "if you wouldn't mind, I'd like to come and buy a cup of coffee to-morrow, like a customer, you know; and I won't let out a word about the stall to the minister next Sunday, don't you be afraid."

She tied the penny carefully into a corner of her rags, and, with a cheerful smile upon her thin face, she glided from under the shadow of the bridge, and was soon lost to Daniel's sight.

Chapter VIII.

An Unexpected Visitor.

 HEN Jessica came to the street into which the court where she lived opened, she saw an unusual degree of excitement among the inhabitants, a group of whom were gathered about a tall gentleman, whom she recognised in an instant to be the minister. She elbowed her way through the midst of them, and the minister's face brightened as she presented herself before him. He followed her up the low entry, across the squalid court, through the stable, empty of the donkeys just then, up the creaking rounds of the ladder, and into the miserable loft, where the tiles were falling in, and the broken window-panes were stuffed with rags and paper. Near to the old rusty stove, which served as a grate when there was any fire, there was a short board laid across some bricks, and upon this the minister took his seat, while Jessica sat upon the floor before him.

"Jessica," he said, sadly, "is this where you live?"

"Yes," she answered, "but we'd a nicer room than this when I was a fairy, and mother played at the theatre; we shall be better off when I'm grown up, if I'm pretty enough to play like her."

"My child," he said, "I'm come to ask your mother to let you go to school in a pleasant place down in the country. Will she let you go?"

"No," answered Jessica; "mother says she'll never let me learn to read, or go to church; it's such a long way off, and she hasn't found me out yet. She always gets very drunk of a Sunday."

The child spoke simply, and as if all she said was a matter of course; but the minister shuddered, and he looked through the broken window to the little patch of gloomy sky overhead.

"What can I do?" he cried mournfully, as though speaking to himself.

"Nothing, please, sir," said Jessica; "only let me come to hear you on a Sunday, and tell me about God. If you was to give me fine clothes like your little girls, mother 'ud only pawn them for gin. You can't do anything more for me."

"Where is your mother?" he asked.

"Out on a spree," said Jessica, "and she won't be home for a day or two. She'd not hearken to you, sir. Once the missionary came, and she pushed him down the ladder, till he was nearly killed. They used to call mother the Vixen at the theatre, and nobody durst say a word to her."

The minister was silent for some minutes, thinking painful thoughts, for his eyes seemed to darken as he looked round the miserable room, and his face wore an air of sorrow and disappointment. At last he spoke again.

"Who is Mr. Daniel, Jessica?" he inquired.

"Oh!" she said cunningly, "he's only a friend of mine as gives me sups of coffee. You don't know all the folks in London, sir!"

"No," he answered, smiling; "but does he keep a coffee-stall?"

Jessica nodded her head, but did not trust herself to speak.

"How much does a cup of coffee cost?" asked the minister.

"A full cup's a penny," she answered promptly; "but you can have half a cup; and there are half-penny and penny buns."

"Good coffee and buns?" he said, with another smile.

"Prime," replied Jessica, smacking her lips.

"Well," continued the minister, "tell your friend to give you a full cup of coffee and a penny bun every morning, and I'll pay for them as often as he chooses to come to me for the money."

Jessica's face beamed with delight, but in an instant it clouded over as she recollected Daniel's secret, and her lips quivered as she spoke her disappointed reply.

"Please, sir," she said, "I'm sure he couldn't come; oh! he couldn't. It's such a long way, and Mr. Dan'el has plenty of customers. No, he never would come to you for the money."

"Jessica," he answered, "I will tell you what I will do. I will trust you with a shilling every Sunday, if you'll promise to give it to your friend the very first time you see him. I shall be sure to know if you cheat me." And the keen, piercing eyes of the minister looked down into Jessica's, and once more the tender and pitying smile returned to his face.

"I can do nothing else for you?" he said, in a tone of mingled sorrow and questioning.

"No, minister," answered Jessica; "only tell me about God."

"I will tell you one thing about Him now," he replied. "If I took you to live in my house with my little daughters, you would have to be washed and clothed in new clothing to make you fit for it. God wanted us to go and live at home with Him in heaven, but we were so sinful that we could never have been fit for it. So He sent His own Son to live among us, and die for us, to wash us from our sins, and to give us new clothing, and to make us ready to live in God's house. When you ask God for anything, you must say, 'For Jesus Christ's sake.' Jesus Christ is the Son of God."

After these words the minister carefully descended the ladder, followed by Jessica's bare and nimble feet, and she led him by the nearest way into one of the great thoroughfares of the city, where he said goodbye to her, adding, "God bless you, my child," in a tone which sank into Jessica's heart. He had put a silver sixpence into her hand to provide for her breakfast the next three mornings, and with a feeling of being very rich, she returned to her miserable home.

The next morning Jessica presented herself proudly as a customer at Daniel's stall, and paid over the sixpence in advance. He felt a little troubled as he heard her story, lest the minister should endeavour to find him out; but he could not refuse to let the child come daily for her comfortable breakfast. If he was detected, he would promise to give up his coffee-stall rather than offend the great people of the chapel; but, unless he was, it would be foolish of him to lose the money it brought in week after week.

Chapter IX.

Jessica's First Prayer Answered.

 VERY Sunday evening the barefooted and bare-headed child might be seen advancing confidently up to the chapel where rich and fashion-able people worshiped God; but before taking her place she arrayed herself in a little cloak and bonnet, which had once belonged to the minister's elder daughter, and which was kept with Daniel's serge gown, so that she presented a somewhat more respectable appearance in the eyes of the congregation.

The minister had no listener more attentive, and he would have missed the pinched, earnest little face, if it were not to be seen in the seat just under the pulpit. At the close of each service he spoke to her for a minute or two in his vestry, often saying no more than a single sentence, for the day's labour had wearied him. The shilling, which was always lying upon the chimney-piece, placed there by Jane and Winny in turns, was immediately handed over, according to promise, to Daniel as she left the chapel, and so Jessica's breakfast was provided for her week after week.

But at last there came a Sunday evening when the minister, going up into his pulpit, did miss the wistful, hungry face, and the shilling lay unclaimed upon the vestry chimney-piece. Daniel looked out for her anxiously every morning, but no Jessica glided into his secluded corner, to sit beside him with her breakfast on her lap, and with a number of strange questions to ask. He felt her absence more keenly than he could have expected. The child was nothing to him, he kept saying to himself; and yet he felt that she was something, and that he could not help being uneasy and anxious about her. Why had he never inquired where she lived? The minister knew, and for a minute Daniel thought he would go and ask him; but that might awaken suspicion. How could he account for so much anxiety, when he was supposed only to know of her absence from chapel one Sunday evening? It would be running a risk, and, after all, Jessica was nothing to him. So he went home and looked over his savings-bank book, and counted his money, and he found, to his satisfaction, that he had gathered together nearly four hundred pounds, and was adding more every week.

But when upon the next Sunday Jessica's seat was again empty, the anxiety of the solemn chapel-keeper overcame his prudence and his fears. The minister had retired to his vestry, and was standing with his arm resting upon the chimney-piece, with his eyes fixed upon the unclaimed shilling, which Winny had laid there before the service, when there was a tap at the door, and Daniel entered with a respectful but hesitating air.

"Well, Standring?" said the minister, questioningly.

"Sir," he said, "I'm uncomfortable about that little girl, and I know you've been once to see after her; she told me about it; and so I make bold to ask you where she lives, and I'll see what has become of her."

"Right, Standring," answered the minister; "I am troubled about the child, and so are my little girls. I thought of going myself, but my time is very much occupied just now."

"I'll go, sir," replied Daniel promptly; and, after receiving the necessary information about Jessica's home, he put out the lights, locked the door, and turned towards his lonely lodgings.

But though it was getting late upon Sunday evening, and Jessica's home was a long way distant, Daniel found that his anxiety would not suffer[10] him to return to his solitary room. It was of no use to reason with himself, as he stood at the corner of the street, feeling perplexed and troubled, and promising his conscience that he would go the very first thing in the morning after he shut up his coffee-stall. In the dim, dusky light, as the summer evening drew to a close, he fancied he could see Jessica's thin figure and wan face gliding on before him, and turning round from time to time to see if he was following. It

---

[10] To allow or permit.

was only fancy, and he laughed a little
at himself; but the laugh was husky,
and there was a choking sensation in
his throat, so he buttoned his Sunday
coat over his chest, where his silver
watch and chain hung temptingly,
and started off at a rapid pace for the
centre of the city.

It was not quite dark when he reached
the court and stumbled up the narrow
entry leading to it; but Daniel did hesi-
tate when he opened the stable door,
and looked into a blank, black space,
in which he could discern nothing. He
thought he had better retreat while he
could do so safely, but as he still stood
with his hand upon the rusty latch, he
heard a faint, small voice through the
nicks of the unceiled boarding above
his head.

"Our Father," said the little voice,
"please to send somebody to me, for
Jesus Christ's sake. Amen."

"I'm here, Jess," cried Daniel, with
a sudden bound of his heart, such as

he had not felt for years, and which almost took away his breath as he peered into the darkness, until at last he discerned dimly the ladder which led up into the loft.

Very cautiously, but with an eagerness which surprised himself, he climbed up the creaking rounds of the ladder and entered the dismal room, where the child was lying in desolate darkness. Fortunately, he had put his box of matches into his pocket, and the end of a wax candle with which he kindled the lamps, and in another minute a gleam of light shone upon Jessica's white features. She was stretched upon a scanty litter of straw under the slanting roof where the tiles had not fallen off, with her poor rags for her only covering; but as her eyes looked upon into Daniel's face bending over her, a bright smile of joy sparkled in them.

"Oh!" she cried gladly, but in a feeble voice, "it's Mr. Dan'el! Has God told you to come here, Mr. Dan'el?"

"Yes," said Daniel, kneeling beside her, taking her wasted hand in his, and parting the matted hair upon her damp forehead.

"What did He say to you, Mr. Dan'el?" said Jessica.

"He told me I was a great sinner," replied Daniel. "He told me I loved a little bit of dirty money better than a poor, friendless, helpless child, whom He had sent to me to see if I would do her a little good for His sake. He looked at me, or the minister did, through and through, and He said, 'Thou fool, this night thy soul shall be required of thee: then whose shall those things be which thou hast provided?' And I could answer Him nothing, Jess. He was come to a reckoning with me, and I could not say a word to Him."

"Aren't you a good man, Mr. Dan'el?" whispered Jessica.

"No, I'm a wicked sinner," he cried, while the tears rolled down his solemn face. "I've been constant at God's house, but only to get money; I've been steady and industrious, but only to get money; and now God looks at me, and He says, 'Thou fool!' Oh, Jess, Jess! you're more fit for heaven than I ever was in my life."

"Why don't you ask Him to make you good for Jesus Christ's sake?" asked the child.

"I can't," he said. "I've been kneeling down Sunday after Sunday when the minister's been praying, but all the time I was thinking how rich some of the carriage people were. I've been loving money and worshipping money all along, and I've nearly let you die rather than run the risk of losing part of my earnings. I'm a very sinful man."

"But you know what the minister often says," murmured Jessica: "'Herein is love, not that we loved God, but that He loved us, and sent His Son to be the propitiation[11] for our sins.'"[12]

---

[11] Atonement or atoning sacrifice.
[12] I John 4:10

"I've heard it so often that I don't feel it," said Daniel. "I used to like to hear the minister say it, but now it goes in at one ear and out at the other. My heart is very hard, Jessica."

By the feeble glimmer of the candle Daniel saw Jessica's wistful eyes fixed upon him with a sad and loving glance; and then she lifted up her weak hand to her face, and laid it over her closed eyelids, and her feverish lips moved slowly.

"God," she said, "please to make Mr. Dan'el's heart soft, for Jesus Christ's sake. Amen."

She did not speak again, nor Daniel, for some time. He took off his Sunday coat and laid it over the tiny shivering frame, which was shaking with cold even in the summer evening; and as he did so he remembered the words which the Lord says He will pronounce at the last day of reckoning: "Inasmuch as ye have done it unto one of the least of these my brethren, ye have done it unto me."[13]

Daniel Standring felt his heart turning with love to the Saviour, and he bowed his head upon his hands, and cried in the depths of his contrite spirit, "God be merciful to me, a sinner."

---

[13] Matthew 25:40b

Chapter X.

The Shadow of Death.

 HERE was no coffee-stall opened under the railway-arch the following morning, and Daniel's regular customers stood amazed as they drew near the empty corner, where they were accustomed to get their early breakfast. It would have astonished them still more if they could have seen how he was occupied

in the miserable loft. He had entrusted
a friendly woman out of the court to
buy food and fuel, and all night long
he had watched beside Jessica, who
was light-headed and delirious, but in
the wanderings of her thoughts and
words, often spoke of God and prayed
for her Mr. Dan'el.

The neighbour informed him that
the child's mother had gone off some
days before, fearing that Jessica was
ill of some infectious fever, and that
she, alone, had taken a little care of
her from time to time. As soon as the
morning came, he sent for a doctor,
and after receiving permission, he
wrapped the poor deserted Jessica in
his coat, and bearing her tenderly in
his arms down the ladder, he carried
her to a cab, which the neighbour
brought to the entrance of the court. It
was to no other than his own solitary
home that he had resolved to take her;
and when the mistress of the lodgings stood at her door, with her arms

a-kimbo,[14] to forbid the admission of the wretched and neglected child, her tongue was silenced by the gleam of a half-sovereign which Daniel slipped into the palm of her hard hand.

By that afternoon's post the minister received the following letter:

Reverend Sir,

If you will condescend to enter under my humble roof, you will have the pleasure of seeing little Jessica, who is at the point of death, unless God in His mercy restores her. Hoping you will excuse this liberty, as I cannot leave the child, I remain, with duty,

Your respectful servant,

D. Standring.

P.S.—Jessica desires her best love and duty to Miss Jane and Winny.

The minister laid aside the book he was reading, and without any delay

---

[14] With hands on hips, and elbows extending outward.

started off for his chapel-keeper's dwelling. There was Jessica lying restfully upon Daniel's bed, but the pinched features were deadly pale, and the sunken eyes shone with a waning light. She was too feeble to turn her head when the door opened, and he paused for a minute, looking at her and at Daniel, who, seated at the head of the bed, was turning over the papers in his desk, and reckoning up once more the savings of his lifetime. But when the minister advanced into the middle of the room, Jessica's white cheeks flushed into a deep red.

"Oh, minister!" she cried, "God has given me everything I wanted except paying Mr. Dan'el for the coffee he used to give me."

"Ah! but God has paid me over and over again," said Daniel, rising to receive the minister. "He's given me my own soul in exchange for it. Let me make bold to speak to you this once, sir. You're a very learned man, and a great preacher, and many people flock to hear you till I'm hard to put it to find seats for them at times; but all the while, hearkening to you every blessed Sabbath, I was losing my soul, and you never once said to me, though you saw me scores and scores of times, 'Standring, are you a saved man?'"

"Standring," said the minister, in a tone of great distress and regret, "I always took it for granted that you were a Christian."

"Ah!" continued Daniel thoughtfully, "but God wanted somebody to ask me that question, and He did not find anybody in the congregation, so He sent this poor little lass to me. Well, I don't mind telling now even if I lose the place; but for a long time, nigh upon ten years, I've kept a coffee-stall on week-days in the city, and cleared, one week with another, about ten shillings: but I was afraid the chapel-wardens wouldn't approve of the coffee business, as low, so I kept

it a close secret and always shut up
early of a morning. It's me that sold
Jessica her cup of coffee, which you
paid for, sir."

"There's no harm in it, my good
fellow," said the minister kindly; "you
need make no secret of it."

"Well," resumed Daniel, "the questions this poor little creature has
asked me have gone quicker and
deeper down to my conscience than
all your sermons, if I may make so
free as to say it. She's come often and
often of a morning, and looked into my
face with those dear eyes of hers, and
said, 'Don't you love Jesus Christ, Mr.
Dan'el? Doesn't it make you very glad
that God is your Father, Mr. Dan'el?
Are we getting nearer heaven every
day, Mr. Dan'el?' And one day says
she, 'Are you going to give all your
money to God, Mr. Dan'el?' Ah! that
question made me think indeed, and
it's never been answered till this day.
While I've been sitting beside the bed

here, I've counted up all my savings, and I've said, 'Lord, it's all Thine; and I'd give every penny of it rather than lose the child, if it be Thy blessed will to spare her life.'"

Daniel's voice quavered at the last words, and his face sank upon the pillow where Jessica's feeble and motionless head lay. There was a very sweet, yet surprised, smile upon her face, and she lifted her wasted fingers to rest upon the bowed head beside her, while she shut her eyes and shaded them with her other weak hand.

"Our Father," she said in a faint whisper, which still reached the ears of the minister and the beadle,[15] "I asked You to let me come home to heaven; but if Mr. Dan'el wants me, please to let me stay a little longer, for Jesus Christ's sake, Amen."

For some minutes after Jessica's prayer there was a deep and unbroken silence in the room, Daniel still

---

[15] A minor parish official once employed in the church to usher and keep order.

hiding his face upon the pillow, and the minister standing beside them with bowed head and closed eyes, as if he also was praying. When he looked up again at the forsaken and desolate child, he saw that her feeble hand had fallen from her face, which looked full of rest and peace, while her breath came faintly, but regularly, through her parted lips. He took her little hand into his own with a pang of fear and grief; but instead of the mortal chillness of death, he felt the pleasant warmth and moisture of life. He touched Daniel's shoulder, and, as he lifted up his head in sudden alarm, he whispered to him, "The child is not dead, but is only asleep."

Before Jessica was fully recovered, Daniel rented a little house for himself and his adopted daughter to dwell in. He made many inquiries after her mother, but she never appeared again in her old haunts, and he was well pleased that there was nobody to interfere with his charge of Jessica. When Jessica grew strong enough, many a cheerful walk had they together, in the early mornings, as they wended their way to the railway-bridge, where the little girl took her place behind the stall, and soon learned to serve the daily customers; and many a happy day was spent in helping to sweep and dust the chapel, into which she had crept so secretly at first, her great delight being to attend to the pulpit and the vestry, and the pew where the minister's children sat, while Daniel and the woman he employed cleaned the rest of the building. Many a Sunday also the minister in his pulpit, and his little daughters in their pew, and Daniel treading softly about the aisles, as their glances fell upon Jessica's eager, earnest, happy face, thought of the first time they saw her sitting amongst the congregation, and of Jessica's first prayer.

My dear friend, may you be a seeker

of God with the innocence and purity of heart as our little barefooted girl, Jessica. Jesus Himself said that unless you become as little children, you cannot enter the kingdom of God.[16] And please do not forget the lesson that we learned from Mr. Dan'el. Store not up for yourselves treasures upon the earth where moth and rust does corrupt, and where thieves break through and steal: but store up for yourselves treasures in heaven. For where your treasure is, there will your heart be also.[17]

For those who seek Him shall find Him, when they search for Him with all their heart.[18]

The End.

---

[16] Referring to Matthew 18:3.
[17] Matthew 6:20-21
[18] Referring to Deuteronomy 4:29 and Jeremiah 29:13.

To Be Continued...

Jessica's First Prayer and *The Rescue of Jessica's Mother* have been adapted into a world-class audio drama entitled *Jessica's Journey*. To view the trailer and learn more about the suspenseful climax, go to:
www.lamplighter.net/jessicas-journey-a-preview

Special Offers

Purchase Lamplighter Theatre's Audio Drama *Jessica's Journey* for $20 (reg. $30) or the digital download for $15 (2 CDs, 2 hours). Use coupon code **JFPSC2013** during checkout to redeem this special offer.

BUY 6 BOOKS - Receive 1 additional book free!

If you enjoyed *Jessica's First Prayer,* you will treasure
these other Lamplighter featured selections.

FOR MOTHERS

A LOST PEARLE
AUTHOR: MRS. GEORGIE SHELDON   PUBLISHED: 1883

Pearle, the beautiful bride, paves the way in a captivating first chapter as, with horror in her eyes, she walks down the aisle. Then her sudden disappearance wreaks havoc, and she is relentlessly pursued. Trials and tragedy often reveal one's true nature, and Pearle comes out shining as she demonstrates great courage and inner strength. She soon realizes that, out of trials that seem to crush us to the earth, we can rise through God's love and help into a purer and better life than we have ever known.

THE LOST CLUE
AUTHOR: MRS. O.F. WALTON   PUBLISHED: 1907

Mrs. Walton had already won our affection as the author of the *Christie* novels, so we launched readily into *The Lost Clue...* and we weren't disappointed. Captain Fortesque, though reared in humble surroundings, is educated in the finest schools of England and finds

himself enjoying the company of the "first circles" until he learns that his father's fortune has evaporated in a risky scheme gone bad. Now, he must make his own way in the world, leaving behind all he thought he knew. But, there is the mystery of a note his dying father left to be read after the funeral, which turns out to be several blank sheets of paper. What can it mean? In the tradition of Jane Austen, Mrs. Walton weaves an intriguing story of honor, duty, family, loss, and redemption.

FOR MOTHERS

THE LAMPLIGHTER
AUTHOR: MARIA S. CUMMINS PUBLISHED: 1854

You'll soon discover why *The Lamplighter* was the third American novel to sell over a million copies! In this poignant novel, poor Gertie

is lying in the snow with a high fever and no one to care for her—until the old lamplighter finds her. This neglected and dejected child experiences loving tenderness as she learns life's lessons and becomes a virtuous young woman. She reciprocates her love by serving her dearest friend when he desperately needs her. *The Lamplighter* is a perfect book for those who long to remain pure of heart. It left such an impression on my life that I decided to name our ministry *Lamplighter Publishing*!

A PEEP BEHIND THE SCENES
AUTHOR: MRS. O.F. WALTON PUBLISHED: 1877

As Rosalie performs on stage the same monotonous acts, the young girls of the village gaze at her with the eyes of admiration and envy. They are certain her life is much more exciting than theirs as they admire her flowing white dress and watch her dance gracefully across the stage. But they do not see what goes on behind the scenes! One day, Rosalie is given hope when an old man gives her a picture of a shepherd who loves her. As she meets hurting people along the way, her new mission is to tell them about the Shepherd who loves them too!

THE HIDDEN HAND
AUTHOR: E.D.E.N. SOUTHWORTH PUBLISHED: 1859

Reader, beware! Once you begin this novel, you will not be able to put

it down! *The Hidden Hand* is strewn with mystery and suspense that will keep you on the edge of your seat from beginning to end. You will find yourself laughing aloud at some of Capitola's antics. But don't let her feisty, mischievous character and Old Hurricane's cantankerous personality derail you from seeing the gracious providence of an all-wise God. His hidden hand can be seen at work in the most difficult situations. *The Hidden Hand* is the book to reach for if you're looking for a good dose of drama and adventure!

FOR MOTHERS AND CHILDREN

TEDDY'S BUTTON
AUTHOR: AMY LEFEUVRE   PUBLISHED: 1896

Here is a story that will open a child's understanding of the spiritual

battle within as Teddy learns that he is his own worst enemy! As a stubborn boy and girl refuse to back down from their selfish pride, one of the many lessons they learn is that they cannot win battles by force and hate, but by carrying the banner of love. Through this charming story, Amy LeFeuvre helps children to understand the spiritual battle that rages in their souls, and that parents and children are on the same side!

THE BASKET OF FLOWERS
AUTHOR: CHRISTOPH VON SCHMID   PUBLISHED: 1823

This first book of the *Lamplighter Rare Collector Series* continues to be a best-seller. James, the king's gardener, teaches his 15-year-old daughter Mary all the principles of godliness through his flowers. She is falsely accused of stealing, and the penalty is death. Mary remembers her father had taught her that it is better to die for the truth than to live for a lie, and that the worst pillow to sleep on is the pillow of a guilty conscience! This story will change your life forever!

THE WHITE DOVE
AUTHOR: CHRISTOPH VON SCHMID

PUBLISHED: 1841

Filled with the intrigue of knights and nobles, thieves and robbers, this is a story of friendship and sacrifice. A little girl agrees to give up her precious white dove to prove her friendship, and lives are miraculously saved.

LITTLE THREADS
AUTHOR: ELIZABETH PRENTISS

PUBLISHED: 1863

It was Mrs. Prentiss' intent that this little gem would be a tool for children to learn obedience. Read about the contrasting lives of Tangle Thread and Golden Thread, one the cause of much grief for her godly mother, and the other the only bright spot in her poor mother's world.

THE LITTLE LAMB

AUTHOR: CHRISTOPH VON SCHMID

PUBLISHED: 1848

While gathering strawberries, ten-year-old Christina finds a shivering lamb that has strayed from its home, and she delights in the thought of caring for it. When confronted with the decision to return it to its rightful owner, her honesty and obedience result in unimagined blessings. Christina learns that even the smallest acts of kindness will bring tremendous joy to herself and to others.

LITTLE SIR GALAHAD

AUTHOR: LILLIAN HOLMES

PUBLISHED: 1904

This story will capture your heart as you peer into the life of a little boy who struggles to walk. Facing new restrictions and challenges, David learns that real strength comes in controlling his own spirit. He seeks to follow the "real" Sir Galahad who said, "My strength is as the strength of ten, because my heart is pure."

HELEN'S TEMPER AND ITS CONSEQUENCES

AUTHOR: MRS. GEORGE GLADSTONE

PUBLISHED: 1872

Unlike her tender-hearted sister, Helen's choices are dictated by fear of what her friends might think if she associates with a girl who is so shabby... so different! Her unchecked temper causes great harm, but God's love proves to be greater than she ever imagined.

JACK THE CONQUEROR

AUTHOR: MRS. C. E. BROWN   PUBLISHED: 1869

No obstacle can daunt Jack's resolve. He has made up his mind to become a useful, honest man and, most of all, to conquer difficulties! His greatest resolve is to learn to read, and he has surmounted obstacles of great magnitude to fulfill his dream. In a secret mountain cave he carries out the craft he learned from the outcast gipsies. Each success emboldens Jack to press on toward higher goals as he plucks up all the courage he can muster to meet life's next challenge!

ROSA OF LINDEN CASTLE

AUTHOR: CHRISTOPH VON SCHMID   PUBLISHED: 1845

When all the trappings of Rosa's life come crashing down around her, the virtues that had been taught to her by her godly parents provide her with direction and guidance even when they are no longer there to walk beside her through the darkened forests. Her love for her father is so complete and selfless that lives are changed and hearts are turned towards good after learning of her incredible act of self-sacrifice. Though she is deserving of so much recognition, she very wisely sends the praise and honor to her heavenly Father whom she loves best of all.

HAND ON THE BRIDLE

AUTHOR: KATHLEEN MACLEOD   PUBLISHED: 1933

The allure of secret sin and the enticement of peer pressure had a strong hold on teens a century ago. Young Gavin knew it was time to venture out beyond his secure environment called home. His longing for independence has become a tainted mixture of stubbornness and pride, but it doesn't take long for him to realize that following the crowd can be risky business. The change that takes place in Gavin's life irritates his friends to the extent that, through vicious threats and heckling taunts, they place him in a predicament that could cost him his life!

THE THREE WEAVERS (ILLUSTRATED)

AUTHOR: REWRITTEN BY MARK HAMBY

Illustrated by Jennifer Brandon

A delightful allegory for fathers to read with their daughters - not just once, but over and over again. This beautifully illustrated rendition reveals how each weaver prepares his daughter to weave a mantle perfectly suited for the prince - and why two suffer the consequences of poor choices while one reaps the benefits of yielding to wise counsel. You will be inspired to enjoy many heart-to-heart talks and thought-provoking conversations together, creating memories for years to come.

TEDDY'S BUTTON (ILLUSTRATED)

AUTHOR: AMY LE FEUVRE
Abridged by Mark Hamby
Illustrated by Jennifer L. Hamby

Young and old alike will love this illustrated re-telling of Lamplighter's best seller! Beautiful illustrations now bring to life a story that is as precious as the one in our original Rare Collector volume. This illustrated version is sure to enlighten younger children and warm the hearts of anyone who reads it. Through this charming story, Amy LeFeuvre helps children to understand the spiritual battle that rages in their souls, and that parents and children are on the same side.

TRUSTY TRIED AND TRUE

AUTHORS: MARK AND DEBBIE HAMBY
Illustrated by Jennifer L. Hamby

The first title in our Trusty collection, this adorable adventure written in the style of Dr. Seuss is bursting with colorful imagery to heighten a child's imagination and stir creativity. Your children will learn much about selfishness, pride, and vanity through the characters of Brawny, Smarty, and Beauty. But most importantly, they will want to be more like Trusty, our hero, who is so eager to help. With self-sacrifice and courage, Trusty is willing to try. You can be sure you'll soon know this story by heart, for it will undoubtedly become a family favorite—to be read over and over and over again!

NEW RELEASE

FROZEN FIRE

AUTHOR: KARL GUSTAV NIERITZ   PUBLISHED: 1834

Based on a true story, Frozen Fire is an action-packed adventure having

the same energy and drama as Teddy's Button. You will fall in love with Betty, whose loyalty and love are demonstrated through tremendous courage and sacrifice. Betty must come face-to-face with the dreaded disease—small pox. Will she save herself? Betty faces myriad trials, including the death-grip of a terrifying blizzard, but the heart-warming love for her devoted servant trumps all. Frozen Fire will keep you on the edge of your seat and will cause you to contemplate the purpose and meaning of life. A provocative read for the entire family!

BUILDING CHARACTER... ONE STORY AT A TIME

A DIVISION OF LAMPLIGHTER MINISTRIES INTERNATIONAL

To order a catalog, call us toll free at 1-888-246-7735,
email us at mail@lamplighter.net,
or visit our website at www.lamplighter.net.

ISBN 978-1-58474-197-8

9 781584 741978

90000 >